The FISH That WASN'T

PAUL BOROVSKY

Hyperion Books for Children
NEW YORK

In a city by the ocean was a brown house. But this was not just any house. It was the house where Paulina lived. Paulina always wore a big bow in her hair.

Across from Paulina's house was a tree-lined park, and there she played with her friends, dug in the sandbox, and basked in the sun.

In the ocean was a large red coral reef. But this was not just any coral reef. This was where the little gray fish lived. The fish swam back and forth through the water, chased other fish, hunted for food, and played in the sand.

One dreary rainy day a rusty old fishing ship headed out of the city's harbor. The fishermen cast their nets into the sea and caught the gray fish. It was unlike any fish they had ever seen and too small to be sold at the market, so they sold it to a pet shop in return for a few silver coins.

That same day was Paulina's birthday, so her mother and father took her to a pet shop. There were animals everywhere. Paulina liked them all, even the creepy spiders, but chose the little gray fish in the corner tank to take home with her. She thought he was neat because he lived underwater. Paulina couldn't stay underwater longer than it took to count to ten.

Paulina named the fish Vincent and set up a bowl for him on her bedside table. That night she fell asleep happy. She dreamed of all her favorite things—Mother and Father and their nice brown house, her friends in the park, all her colorful bows arranged neatly in her dresser drawer, and most of all, her new little fish.

Vincent wasn't feeling quite as happy to find himself in a small fishbowl. He dreamed of the big blue ocean, of shells in the sand, and of the bright red coral reef he called home.

After awhile, Paulina noticed something odd about Vincent's fishbowl. It seemed to have gotten smaller! So Paulina moved Vincent to the bathroom sink. And it wasn't long before the sink seemed to have shrunk, too, so she put Vincent into the bathtub.

Vincent was definitely getting bigger. Was he eating too much? Nobody was sure. He grew so big that the bathtub soon collapsed from his weight. Paulina and her parents carried him into the backyard and put him into the pool, where he fit just fine—for the time being, at least.

Paulina brought her toys out to the pool so they could play together. They tossed balls to each other and sailed boats on the water. Sometimes Paulina made Vincent laugh when she tied one of her colorful bows on his tail. But the most fun they had was when they peeked over the garden wall at people passing by.

At the end of each day Paulina read Vincent a story from her favorite picture book. In return, as Paulina drifted off to sleep, Vincent would sing to her. People from the whole neighborhood would stop to listen. "I wonder why the songs sound so sad?" they would ask one another.

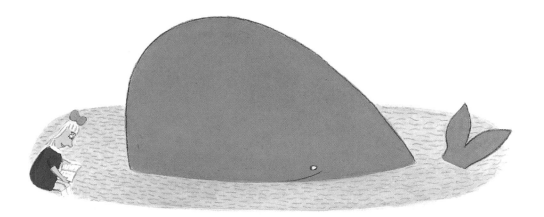

One morning when Father was taking out the garbage, he saw Vincent doing something very strange. He was spraying water out of his head. It reminded Father of something, so he dropped the garbage and ran to the library. He looked through some books about ocean animals and found a picture that looked just like Vincent.

"Oh my goodness," he cried. "Vincent isn't a fish — he's a whale!" He raced back to the pool and told Paulina, "We can't keep Vincent in our swimming pool. He's going to get really big. A small fish in a large bowl is one thing, but a large whale in a small pool is quite another!"

Father and Paulina put Vincent in the car and drove him down the block along the tree-lined park. Past cafés and tall buildings, they drove through the winding streets until they came to the ocean. There they set Vincent free. Vincent, happy to be back at the coral reef, flipped his tail on the surface and dived deep in the water for shells. He was home again.

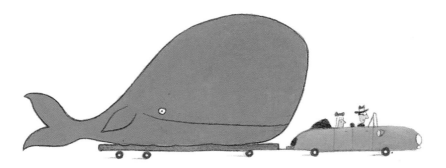

When Paulina and Father returned home, Paulina went and sat by the pool. She wished Vincent could have stayed. She was so upset that she began to cry. She cried all day and cried all night. In the morning she woke still crying and cried as she walked to school. She cried through the park and down the streets. She cried so much that she couldn't see through her tears. She passed the school and didn't even notice when she got to the end of a pier and fell right into the ocean.

"Help!" she screamed, when she realized she couldn't touch the bottom. All she could do was take a deep breath before she started to sink. She looked around and saw a beautiful underwater world — colorful coral and shells, plants waving in the current, crabs digging in the sand, and hundreds and hundreds of sparkling fish. It didn't look like the world she knew at all.

Paulina couldn't hold her breath any longer. She splashed and gasped and kicked and wiggled. She was growing tired, but the pier was out of reach. Just when she thought she would sink to the bottom of the ocean, something lifted her from underneath and gently placed her on the pier. Vincent!

Paulina took a deep breath. It felt good to have the earth beneath her feet and to feel the sun warming her back. She had to admit that Vincent looked happy swimming in the ocean. She even thought he appeared small again with all the water around him.

"Good-bye, Vincent," she said. He smiled, then dived back into the ocean, where he danced and sprayed for her in the setting sun.

Paulina turned around and headed home, but not before taking one last look at Vincent as he swam away through the vast water that lay before him.

Thereafter when Paulina walked along the shore she would sometimes hear the distant songs of whales. "Vincent is singing a song for me," she would say. "A happy song!"

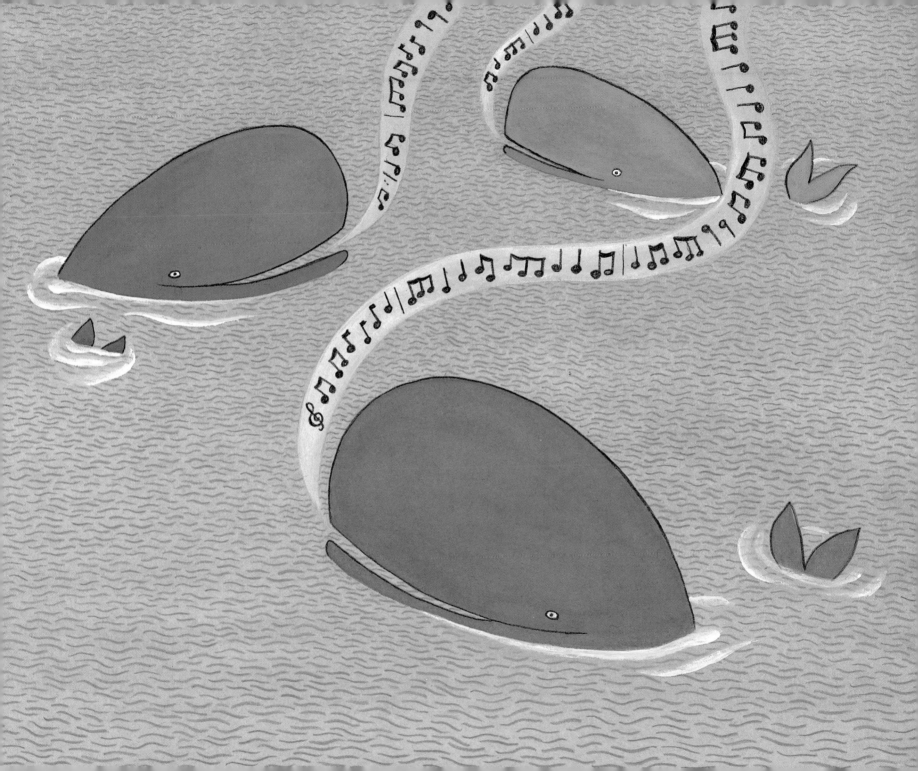

Text and illustrations ©1994 by Paul Borovsky.
All rights reserved. Printed in Singapore.
For information address Hyperion Books for Children,
114 Fifth Avenue, New York, New York 10011.
FIRST EDITION
1   3   5   7   9   10   8   6   4   2

Library of Congress Cataloging-in-Publication Data
Borovsky, Paul.
The fish that wasn't/Paul Borovsky — 1st ed.
p.   cm.
Summary: A little girl learns that every creature has its own place
when she gets a strange gray fish for her birthday.
ISBN 1-56282-581-X (trade) — ISBN 1-56282-582-8 (lib. bdg.)
[1. Fishes — Fiction. 2. Pets — Fiction. 3. Whales — Fiction.]
I. Title.
PZ7.B64849Fi 1994
[E] — dc20   93-11680   CIP   AC

The artwork for each picture is prepared using
watercolor and gouache.
This book is set in 18-point Memphis Medium.